118557

96

SUPERMOO!

Babette Cole

BBC BOOKS

Most people think cows are
boring old munchers . . .

Well, this one isn't . . .

Down in the Cowcave her friend,
Calf Crypton, works
the cowputer.

BOTS operating in channel. Spreading smelly fog. Treacle Tankers in collision!

MESSAGE FROM COWPEACE
BoTs: BoTs:
BoTs: BoTs:
Help!

When there is a world disaster they
are the first to know.
"Crikey cream cheese!" said Calf Crypton.
"This message is
important!"

When Supermoo was plugged into the cowputer her supervision could flash up what was happening. "Suffering silage," said Supermoo, "it's the devilish **BOTS!**"

There was no time to lose!
They sped out to sea.

The Bots, evil spreaders of filth and pollution, were making a smelly fog with their Bot pipes.

BLUB

BLUB

BLUBBER

FIZ FUT FUT

BANG!

The fog caused two treacle tankers to smack into each other. There was treacle everywhere!

Supermoo bashed the Bots.

"Keep our country green and clean, you dirty things!" said Supermoo.

Supermoo and Calf Crypton saved the crews
by picking up the tankers with their
magnetic hoofs.

They zoomed towards the shore.

They flew the tankers to the docks
to be mended.

On the beach, Miss Pimple's class was having a swimming lesson.

The treacle slick from the crash was coming straight for them!

Supermoo blew
a huge
bubble.

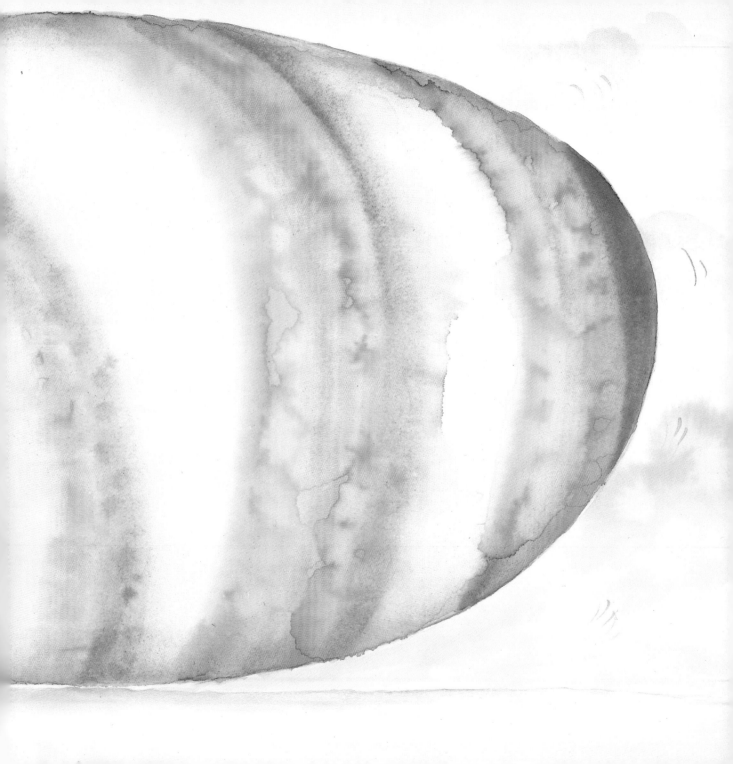

They rolled the bubble in
the treacle.

All the treacle stuck to it.
Supermoo and
Calf Crypton
carried it
away.

Miss Pimple's class was saved!

Then a message came through on
their electronic ear-pieces.
It was from the
United
Nations!

"Frying flies!" said Supermoo.

An oil-well was on fire and had
to be put out.

Supermoo and Calf Crypton flew the
treacle bubble towards
the blazing well.

SIZZLE

When they were over the well Supermoo popped the bubble with her horns.

All the treacle
went down the well
and put out the fire.

It was so hot it turned into a giant
toffee tube.

Miss Pimple's class had toffee
for ever.

"Put the paper in a bin," said Supermoo.

On the way home someone called them with the "Cowsign".
Could it be another cowbusting crime to crack . . . ?

No! It was time
to deliver the
milk . . .

. . . in the Cowmobile!

SUPERMOO was first shown on the
BBC School TV series
Words and Pictures

Published by BBC Books,
a division of BBC Enterprises Limited,
Woodlands, 80 Wood Lane, London W12 0TT
First published 1992
© Babette Cole 1992
ISBN 0 563 36366 5

Set in 20/24pt Baskerville
by Goodfellow & Egan, Cambridge
Printed and bound in Belgium by
Proost NV